## Here's what kids have to say about reading Magic Tree House® books and Magic Tree House® Merlin Missions:

*Thank you for writing these great books! I have learned a great deal of information about history and the world around me.*—Rosanna

*Your series, the Magic Tree House, was really influential on my late childhood years. [Jack and Annie] taught me courage through their rigorous adventures and profound friendship, and how they stuck it out through thick and thin, from start to finish.*—Joe

*Your description is fantastic! The words pop out... oh, man... [the Magic Tree House series] is really exciting!*—Christina

*I like the Magic Tree House series. I stay up all night reading them. Even on school nights!*—Peter

*I think I've read about twenty-five of your Magic Tree House books! I'm reading every Magic Tree House book I can get my hands on!*—Jack

*Never stop writing, and if you can't think about anything to write about, don't worry, use some of my ideas!!*—Kevin

## Parents, teachers, and librarians love Magic Tree House® books, too!

*[Magic Tree House] comes up quite a bit at parent/teacher conferences.... The parents are amazed at how much more reading is being done at home because of your books. I am very pleased to know such fun and interesting reading exists for students.... Your books have also made students want to learn more about the places Jack and Annie visit. What wonderful starters for some research projects!*—Kris L.

*As a librarian, I have seen many happy young readers coming into the library to check out the next Magic Tree House book in the series. I have assisted young library patrons with finding nonfiction materials related to the Magic Tree House book they have read. . . . The message you are sending to children is invaluable: siblings can be friends; boys and girls can hang out together. . . .*—Lynne H.

*[My daughter] had a slow start reading, but somehow with your Magic Tree House series, she has been inspired and motivated to read. It is with such urgency that she tracks down your books. She often blurts out various facts and lines followed by "I read that in my Magic Tree House book."*—Jenny E.

*[My students] seize every opportunity they can to reread a Magic Tree House book or look at all the wonderful illustrations. Jack and Annie have opened a door to a world of literacy that I know will continue throughout the lives of my students.*—Deborah H.

*[My son] carries his Magic Tree House books everywhere he goes. He just can't put the book he is reading down until he finishes it. . . . He is doing better in school overall since he has made reading a daily thing. He even has a bet going with his aunt that if he continues doing well in school, she will continue to buy him the next book in the Magic Tree House series.* —Rosalie R.

# MAGIC TREE HOUSE® #45
## A MERLIN MISSION

# A Crazy Day
## with Cobras

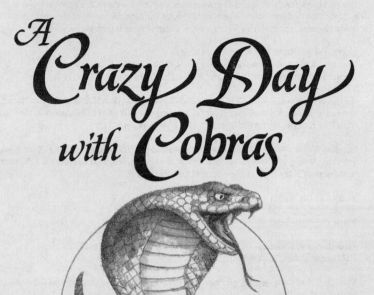

by Mary Pope Osborne

illustrated by Sal Murdocca

## A STEPPING STONE BOOK™

Random House 🏠 New York

Text copyright © 2011 by Mary Pope Osborne
Cover art and interior illustrations copyright © 2011 by Sal Murdocca
Sticker illustrations copyright © 2012 by Sal Murdocca

All rights reserved. Published in the United States by Random House Children's Books, a division of Random House, Inc., New York. Originally published in hardcover in the United States by Random House Children's Books, New York, in 2011.

Random House and the colophon are registered trademarks and A Stepping Stone Book and the colophon are trademarks of Random House, Inc. Magic Tree House is a registered trademark of Mary Pope Osborne; used under license.

Visit us on the Web!
randomhouse.com/kids
MagicTreeHouse.com

Educators and librarians, for a variety of teaching tools, visit us at
RHTeachersLibrarians.com

The Library of Congress has cataloged the hardcover edition of this work as follows:
Osborne, Mary Pope.
A crazy day with cobras / by Mary Pope Osborne ; illustrated by Sal Murdocca. — 1st ed.
   p.  cm. — (Magic tree house ; #45)
"A Merlin mission."
"A Stepping Stone book."
Summary: The magic tree house whisks Jack and Annie back to India during the Mogul Empire in the 1600s to search for an emerald needed to break a magic spell.
ISBN 978-0-375-86823-8 (trade) — ISBN 978-0-375-96823-5 (lib. bdg.) —
ISBN 978-0-375-89875-4 (ebook)
[1. Time travel—Fiction. 2. Tree houses—Fiction. 3. Magic—Fiction.
4. Brothers and sisters—Fiction. 5. India—History—1526–1765—Fiction.]
I. Murdocca, Sal, ill. II. Title.
PZ7.O81167Cr 2011 [Fic]—dc22 2010013896

ISBN 978-0-375-86795-8 (pbk.)

Printed in the United States of America

10 9 8 7 6 5 4 3

5571 2375
8/14

*For Nikita, Kumar, and Susan*

# Dear Reader,

*The hottest day of my life was also the day I saw the most beautiful building of my life. Many years ago, friends and I rode for months in a van, traveling through Asia. When we arrived in Agra, India, the heat was so unbearable I could barely think or move. A tour guide led us around to see the sights, and late in the afternoon, we arrived at one of the wonders of the world: the Taj Mahal.*

*When I got out of the van, I forgot all about the heat. I felt as if I had stepped from the real world into a dream. Through the heat waves, a twenty-story marble building shimmered in the pink twilight. The Taj Mahal was the tomb of a Mogul queen named Mumtāz Mahal, built by her grieving husband, Shah Jahān, in the 1600s.*

*Since that day, I've always wanted to go back to the Taj Mahal. In this book, traveling with Jack and Annie, I finally have.*

*Thanks for joining us.*

Mary Pope Osborne

# CONTENTS

*Only let this one teardrop,*
*the Taj Mahal, glisten spotlessly bright*
*on the cheek of time, forever and ever.*
—Rabindranath Tagore,
Nobel laureate poet from West Bengal

# Prologue

One summer day in Frog Creek, Pennsylvania, a mysterious tree house appeared in the woods. It was filled with books. A boy named Jack and his sister, Annie, soon discovered that the tree house was magic, and just by pointing at a book, they could go to any time and any place in history. And while they were gone, no time at all passed back in Frog Creek.

Jack and Annie eventually found out that the tree house belonged to Morgan le Fay, a magical librarian from the legendary realm of Camelot. They have since traveled on many adventures in the magic tree house and have completed many missions for both Morgan le Fay and Merlin the magician. On these journeys, they've often received help from two young enchanters from Camelot named Teddy and Kathleen.

Now Jack and Annie are waiting to hear about where they will be going next—for their forty-fifth adventure in the magic tree house.

## CHAPTER ONE

## A Terrible Mistake

"The weather's getting warmer," said Jack. He and Annie were walking home from school under a cloudless May sky. A warm breeze blew through the leaves on the newly green trees.

"I love it," said Annie. "It makes me feel like something good's going to happen."

"Something good already happened," said Jack. "My teacher finally gave back my story today."

"The one about our adventures in the tree house?" asked Annie.

"Yep. She said I have a fantastic imagination," said Jack.

"Great!" said Annie.

"And she loved your drawings for the story, too," said Jack. "She said you're really talented."

"That's nice!" said Annie. "Maybe she loved the sparkle pens I used."

"The only thing she didn't love was the type I chose," said Jack. "She said it was hard to read because it was too fancy."

"I really like that curly type," said Annie.

"Me too," said Jack. "But it's no big deal—she still gave me an A plus."

"Wow, cool," said Annie.

As they reached the edge of the Frog Creek woods, a gust of wind shook the tree branches. Jack's baseball cap blew off. He grabbed his cap from the sidewalk. The wind blew harder.

"What's happening?" said Annie.

Suddenly two figures rushed out of the woods. Their dark cloaks flapped behind them as they hurried toward Jack and Annie.

"Teddy!" said Annie.

"Kathleen!" said Jack.

The red-haired teenage boy and the beautiful girl with dark wavy hair ran to Jack and Annie and hugged them.

"You must come with us to the tree house!" said Kathleen. "Hurry!"

"Why? What's up?" said Jack.

"We'll explain when we get there!" said Teddy. He and Kathleen turned and started back into the woods. As Jack and Annie raced after them, sunlight slanted through the leafy treetops.

Soon they all came to the tallest oak tree. "Up, up!" cried Teddy.

One by one, Teddy, Kathleen, Jack, and Annie scrambled up the rope ladder and climbed into the magic tree house. When they were all inside, Teddy heaved a sigh. "My friends, we desperately need your help," he said.

"What's wrong?" asked Annie.

"We made a terrible mistake!" said Kathleen.

"No, it was me, just me," said Teddy. "I made the mistake."

"What did you do?" said Jack.

"I turned Penny into a stone statue," said Teddy.

"Penny?" said Annie. "A statue?"

"Oh, no," said Jack. He loved the little orphan penguin that he and Annie had found on one of their adventures. Penny had helped save Merlin's life.

"It was an accident," said Kathleen.

"It was stupidity!" said Teddy. "We were in Morgan's library, and I was looking at spells in her books. Morgan forbids us to try any spells on our own, but I disobeyed when I found a simple one that turns things into stone. I thought I'd just give it a quick try—I turned an apple, a goblet of water, and a writing quill all to stone!"

"Teddy was pointing at a walking stick by the doorway, reciting the words of the spell," said Kathleen. "And just as he finished, Penny wandered in, and the spell hit *her*!"

"And now she's a stone statue," Teddy said miserably.

"That's terrible," said Annie.

"Well, can't you just ask Merlin or Morgan to use their magic to bring Penny back to life?" asked Jack.

"No, no, they must never learn anything about this! If they do, I . . ." Teddy shook his head and looked away.

"Merlin and Morgan are both in Avalon for the Festival of May," said Kathleen. "If they discover what Teddy has done, we fear Merlin will banish him from the kingdom."

"Really?" said Annie.

"Yes, Merlin will be enraged," said Kathleen. "Penny is the very heart of our kingdom. We all love her very much."

"Me too," said Jack. He thought about the penguin's fuzzy head, the funny way she peeped, the way she loved and trusted everyone.

"The good news is that we have found a rhyme that tells us how to reverse the stone spell," said Kathleen. She took a note from her cloak.

"The bad news is that it is written in an ancient

language," said Teddy. "We have only translated eight lines so far."

Kathleen read from the note:

> *Ye say that ye wish*
> *your spell be reversed?*
> *Four things ye must find.*
> *Here is the first:*

> *In the shape of a rose*
> *is an emerald stone*
> *that uncovers the heart*
> *of one who's alone.*

"An emerald stone shaped like a rose?" said Jack. He took the note from Kathleen and looked at it. "That's what you have to find first?"

"Yes, only *we* must spend our time trying to translate the rest of the spell before Merlin and Morgan return," said Kathleen, "so we need you and Annie to look for the emerald rose."

"Got it," said Jack.

"Where do we look?" asked Annie.

"We have done some research," said Teddy, "and we think you should go back almost four hundred years and visit one of the Great Moguls of India."

"Great Moguls?" said Annie.

"They are the emperors who ruled India's Mogul Empire," said Teddy. "One of them had the largest collection of precious gems in all the world."

"And his stonecutters cut many of his jewels into the shape of leaves and flowers!" said Kathleen.

"Perfect!" said Annie.

"Our research says he often gave gifts of his precious gems to visiting ambassadors," said Teddy. "You will have to pretend to be ambassadors."

"And I am afraid, Annie, that you will have to pretend to be a boy again," said Kathleen. "In Mogul India, girls were not allowed to show their faces in public."

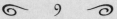

"No problem, I'm getting used to it," Annie said.

"Wait, even if Annie's a boy, they're probably not going to believe that we're ambassadors," said Jack.

Teddy and Kathleen gave each other blank looks. "I do not know why not," said Teddy, "though I admit we do not really know very much about ambassadors."

"They're people who visit other countries to represent their own country," said Jack.

"Splendid!" said Teddy. "So that's what you'll do—you'll represent Frog Creek four hundred years ago."

"Except ambassadors are usually grown-ups," said Jack.

"Oh. Well. I suppose you must just do the best you can," said Kathleen.

"Perhaps *this* will help you," said Teddy. "If you have knowledge, you will seem older." He reached into his cloak and pulled out a book.

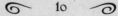

"And we thought perhaps some magic might help, too," said Kathleen, "if you find yourselves in danger." She reached into her cloak again and pulled out a tiny blue bottle. "A potion to make you very small."

"Wow, great!" said Annie.

"Uh . . . very small?" said Jack. He remembered how their friend Augusta had been made tiny by the fairies of Ireland. He remembered that he'd been afraid it might happen to them, too. All kinds of ordinary things could seem huge and scary, he thought. "How long would we stay small?" he asked.

"It depends on how many sips you take," said Kathleen, giving the bottle to Jack. "One sip will make you small for ten minutes, two for twenty, three for thirty, and so on."

"Thanks," he said. He put the bottle and the rhyme into his backpack.

"Go now," said Teddy. "Find the emerald rose while we try to translate the rest of the spell."

"We'll do our best," said Annie.

"Thank you," said Kathleen. "When you need strength, just think of Penny."

"We will," said Jack. He took a deep breath and pointed at the cover of their research book. "I wish we could go *there*!"

Annie waved at Teddy and Kathleen. "See you later!" she said.

The wind started to blow.

The tree house started to spin.

It spun faster and faster.

Then everything was still.

Absolutely still.

# CHAPTER TWO

# The Red Fort

Kathleen and Teddy were gone. The air was hot. Flies buzzed around Jack's head.

"*These* are ambassador clothes?" said Annie.

Jack and Annie were dressed alike. They both wore wide-brimmed felt hats, stockings, buckled shoes, short jackets, and puffy short pants. Jack's backpack had turned into a leather bag.

"I guess," said Jack. "This must be how we would've dressed almost four hundred years ago in Frog Creek."

"If we'd both been boys," said Annie. "So, where are we?"

Jack and Annie looked out the window. The tree house had landed in a row of tall dark trees. The trees stood next to a red fort with a moat, a drawbridge, and massive red battlements.

"Cool fort," said Jack.

"Yeah, and look—elephants," said Annie. "I love elephants!"

Leading away from the fort were two streets. One was filled with oxen pulling carts and people riding horses and elephants. Veiled women sat in carriages on the elephants' backs.

"Yeah, and there's a bazaar like the one we saw in Baghdad," said Jack. He pointed to the other street, which was lined with tents and stalls.

"So where do you think we find an emerald stone in the shape of a rose?" said Annie.

Jack picked up their research book and opened to the first page. He read aloud:

In the 1600s, India was a vast land of crowded cities and countless villages. A great deal of India, though, was still covered by wilderness. Wild creatures such as cheetahs, elephants, and Bengal tigers lived in its forests. India's wilderness was also home for many snakes, including the king cobra, one of the deadliest snakes on earth.

"Yikes," said Annie. She and Jack looked at pictures of a Bengal tiger and a king cobra. The growling tiger had a huge head and enormous teeth. The cobra had speckled yellow bands around its long body. Its open jaws revealed two deadly fangs.

"Don't worry," said Jack with a shiver. "We definitely didn't land in the wilderness." He turned the pages until he found a drawing of the red fort. "Yes! Here's exactly where we landed." He read:

> For several centuries, mighty rulers, known as Great Moguls, ruled over much of India. The wealthiest of the Great Moguls was named Shah Jahān. He lived inside the Red Fort, where he was protected night and day by imperial guards.

"So the Great Mogul lives right here!" said Annie. "How lucky is that?"

She and Jack looked at the fort again. "I guess those guys must be imperial guards," Jack said. He pointed to men in white coats and leggings guarding the drawbridge. Some carried spears; others had bows and arrows.

"Right. But who do you think *those* guys are?" Annie asked, pointing. Two carts pulled by pairs of white oxen had stopped at the entrance to the bridge. Eight men were climbing out of the carts. They wore outfits like Jack's and Annie's—puffy pants, short jackets, and wide hats. Two of the guards greeted them with deep bows.

"They're dressed like us," said Jack. "So I guess they must be ambassadors, too."

"If they're visiting the Great Mogul, we should join them!" said Annie.

"Hold on," said Jack. He opened his bag. As he put their book inside, he noticed that everything that had been in his backpack was still there: his story from school, the note about the emerald rose, and the blue bottle with the potion to make them small. "Okay, we've got everything," he said.

"Come on, before we miss our chance!" Annie called, starting down the rope ladder.

"Wait!" said Jack. He put his bag over his shoulder and hurried after Annie. By the time he stepped off the ladder, Annie was already heading toward the drawbridge of the fort.

"Annie, hold on! We have to talk about something important!" said Jack. He didn't want her to say anything crazy to the guards or the ambassadors.

"What?" said Annie, waiting for him.

"If they're real ambassadors, we shouldn't get too close to them," Jack said. "They'll figure out we're fakes."

"Oh. Good point," said Annie.

"So let's wait until they start across the bridge," said Jack. "Then we'll run to the gate and tell the guards that we're supposed to be with them. And don't forget, if anyone asks, you're my brother. Oh, you should stick your braids under your hat."

"Right," said Annie. She tucked her pigtails under her hat. "How's that?"

"Fine, I guess," said Jack. He was still worried about the fact that he and Annie looked too young. "We have to try to act like ambassadors. So stand up straight and speak in a low voice."

"Okay, don't worry," said Annie.

"And we should hold up our chins," said Jack. "Try to look taller."

"Okay, okay. Oh, look, they're leaving," said Annie. "Let's go!"

The ambassadors had climbed back into their oxcarts. As the carts started across the moat, Jack and Annie walked quickly toward the bridge.

The first guard held up his spear. "Who are you?" he asked. He had a long purple scar on his cheek and silver rings in his ears.

"We are ambassadors," Jack said in a deep voice. "We are with the gentlemen who just crossed the bridge."

The guard gave Jack and Annie a sharp look. "You are with the ambassadors from Europe?" he said.

"Yes"—Jack stood straighter—"but we're from Frog Creek."

"I imagine you are thinking that we look very young," Annie said in a low voice. "Well, it is true, we *are* young. But we are very learned."

"I see," said the guard.

"And imaginative and creative," Annie added.

*Oh, brother*, thought Jack.

"I see," said the guard again. He looked at Jack's bag. "And is that where you carry your treasure? Your gifts for the Great Mogul?"

"Um ... well ... ," said Jack.

"What gifts do ambassadors from Europe usually give Great Moguls?" Annie asked.

"The gifts sent by the kings and queens of Europe are always rare and beautiful," said the guard.

"Such as ... ?" said Annie.

"Silver swords, golden goblets, treasure chests filled with jewels and coins," said the guard, "or perhaps ... the fastest horses from Arabia."

*Forget it*, thought Jack.

But Annie smiled. "I see," she said. "Well, I am pleased to tell you that *we* have brought a gift far greater than *any* of those things."

# CHAPTER THREE

## Complete Respect

"**V**ery good!" the guard said. "The Great Mogul eagerly awaits your arrival—and your treasure!"

*What treasure?* thought Jack. *What is Annie talking about?*

"You may pass through the gate," said the guard. "Follow the other ambassadors to the Hall of Public Audience, where the Great Mogul appears each morning before his court nobles."

"Thanks!" said Annie. She pulled Jack along toward the drawbridge.

"And do not worry," the guard called after

them. "The Great Mogul will not mind your youth. His grandfather became emperor when he was thirteen."

"Super! Thanks!" Annie called back.

"Hey, what were you talking about back there?" Jack whispered as he and Annie started across the bridge. "We didn't bring any treasure for the Great Mogul! We didn't bring anything!"

"Yes, we did," said Annie.

"What? Tell me what," said Jack.

"Your story," said Annie. "It's in your bag, right?"

"You've got to be kidding!" said Jack. "That's not treasure!"

"Yes, it is! Think about it! You printed your story in fancy curly type from the computer, right?" said Annie. "I did my drawings with sparkle pens. There were no computers or sparkle pens four hundred years ago! The Great Mogul has never seen writing and artwork like that. Our ordinary stuff would be *treasure* in his time!"

"I—I don't know. . . ." Jack didn't know what to think. He just shook his head.

"It would be! Trust me," said Annie. "And hurry! We don't want to lose the other ambassadors!" She ran to the entrance of the Red Fort.

Jack followed her. They passed through a gateway that opened onto a stone road. The road led to a large square. At the opposite side of the square was a long, low building with columns and arches.

"There they are," said Annie. She pointed to the ambassadors' oxcarts rolling toward the building.

"That must be the Hall of Public Audience," said Jack.

Jack and Annie walked quickly toward the building. The air felt as if it were coming from a hot furnace. By the time they arrived at the hall, Jack felt faint from the heat.

The ambassadors from Europe had already gone inside. Fierce-looking guards stood at all the entrances. Daggers and curved swords hung from their belts.

Annie walked up to one of the burly guards. "Excuse me," she said in a low voice, "but we are ambassadors from Frog Creek, and we are supposed to be with those other ambassadors."

To Jack's surprise, the guard asked no questions. He nodded and gestured for them to follow him.

Annie and Jack followed the guard into the shadowy hall. The air inside was much cooler. It smelled of roses and mint. Hidden musicians played soft music.

The burly guard escorted Jack and Annie past the audience of court nobles. All the men had beards or mustaches and wore beautiful coats of many colors and patterns—bright orange, purple, turquoise, green striped, and pale pink with flowers.

Next to the nobles, the eight ambassadors from Europe stood along a silver railing. They were lined up in pairs. The burly guard ushered Jack and Annie to the end of the line.

Everyone in the hall was facing a high platform with wide steps. The platform was made of

sparkling diamonds, emeralds, and pearls. Gold columns supported a golden canopy above the platform. Statues of two jeweled peacocks with rubies in their beaks were perched above the canopy. Over the golden canopy was another canopy of rich cloth.

Tall, thin candlesticks held flickering candles, and servants sprayed rose-scented water into the air. As Annie looked around at everything, Jack slipped their book out of his bag. He huddled over it and read to himself.

Every morning, the Great Mogul sat on his Peacock Throne in the Hall of Public Audience. He demanded complete respect. Everyone had to be perfectly still and silent in his presence. No one was allowed to sit or leave as long as he was in the hall. If his guests spoke to him without permission or did not bow the proper way, he could have them killed.

*Oh, man!* thought Jack. He shoved the book back into his bag and turned to Annie. "Don't speak!" he whispered. "And we have to bow the proper way!"

"Don't worry, we learned how to bow in the palace in Vienna," Annie said.

"No, this is different!" whispered Jack. "When I messed up *there*, people just laughed. *Here*, they kill you!"

"Oh. Well, don't forget we've got our potion from Kathleen," Annie whispered. "If worse comes to worst, we can make ourselves small and escape."

"Forget it," Jack whispered. "I don't want to be a tiny little person! The guards will just chase us down and squash us like bugs!"

Annie laughed.

"This isn't funny," said Jack. "Let's go back outside and make another plan. We don't know what we're doing here."

"Yes, we do," Annie said. "We're going to give your story to the Great Mogul, and then we're going to ask him for an emerald rose. Simple."

"No, no!" said Jack. "I told you we can't say a word to him! Not a word! Come on, we have to leave while we're still alive."

Annie sighed. "Okay, fine," she said.

But as Jack and Annie turned to go, trumpet blasts shattered the air. The trumpet sounds were followed by deafening drumrolls.

Shah Jahān, the Great Mogul of India, stepped through a door at the back of the hall.

# CHAPTER FOUR

# The Great Mogul

Jack and Annie froze. The hall was completely still and silent. The Great Mogul climbed the steps to the Peacock Throne. He wore an orange turban and a silver coat trimmed with diamonds and pearls. He wore ropes of jewels around his neck and sparkling rings on his fingers.

The Great Mogul sat cross-legged on a cushion and looked coldly at his audience. He had a handsome face with a sharp nose and dark, distant eyes. A servant stood near him, waving a large peacock-feather fan. Another waved a broom to shoo away flies.

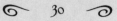

An imperial guard escorted a pair of European ambassadors up the wide steps that led to the throne.

Jack and Annie watched carefully as the ambassadors stood before the Great Mogul. The two men bowed from their waists and brushed the back of their right hands over the carpet. They straightened up, raised their right hands into the air, and placed their palms on top of their heads. Then they lowered their hands and stood very still.

*So that's the way to bow before a Great Mogul,* thought Jack. He hoped he and Annie could remember how to do it.

One of the ambassadors then opened a bag and pulled out a jewel-studded crown and a golden goblet. He gave them to the Great Mogul. The ruler looked at the glittering gifts. Without smiling, he handed them to a servant who had appeared beside him.

Another servant stepped forward with a silver tray. On the tray was a red satin pillow. Spread across the pillow were dozens of glittering jewels. The ambassadors selected several precious gems. Then they turned and walked slowly down the steps of the throne.

Annie nudged Jack. He looked at her, and she smiled. He knew just what she was thinking: *Those guys got jewels without saying a word!*

But Jack was still worried. An emerald rose wasn't an ordinary jewel. Plus, his story seemed like such a teeny gift compared to a crown and a gold goblet.

The other ambassadors climbed the Peacock Throne in pairs. They all bowed in the same way. They all opened their bags and gave gifts to the Great Mogul—a carved wooden clock, a crystal necklace, a gleaming silver sword. As the ruler received each exquisite gift, he never changed his expression.

Jack grew more and more anxious. If the Great Mogul seemed bored with *these* treasures, what would he think of a kid's story?

All the ambassadors from Europe were offered

jewels from the silver tray. Then they resumed their place in line. Finally an imperial guard beckoned to Jack and Annie. It was their turn!

Jack's legs felt wobbly as he walked with Annie up the steps of the throne. The Great Mogul looked at them with his distant, cold stare.

Together, Jack and Annie bowed from their waists. They brushed the back of their right hands over the carpet. They stood up and raised their right hands into the air. They placed their palms on top of their heads. Jack held his breath the whole time. A fly landed on his nose, but he didn't flinch.

Jack and Annie lowered their arms. Jack's hands were shaky as he unbuckled his bag and pulled out his story. Without a word, he handed it to the Great Mogul.

The ruler stared at the first page. Slowly he ran his fingers over the fancy type. He turned the page and stared at Annie's sparkly drawing of the tree house in the Frog Creek woods. Again he touched the page.

Then the Great Mogul raised his eyes and looked straight at Jack and Annie. The next thing Jack knew, the servant was standing in front of them with the tray of jewels. In a panic, Jack stared at the pile of diamonds, pearls, and red, green, and yellow gems. The jewels were all cut in different shapes.

*Emerald rose!* Jack thought wildly. He tried to focus, but the glittering gems swirled in front of his eyes—flowers, fish, stars, birds, butterflies, pears, and apples. But no emerald rose!

When Jack glanced up, he saw the Great Mogul watching him. Jack was ready to grab anything!

Annie reached forward and carefully picked up a green stone. She solemnly showed it to Jack. *It was a small emerald shaped like a rose!*

Jack nodded, trying to appear calm. His heart was pounding. He glanced at the Great Mogul. The ruler was looking at them with interest. He seemed about to say something. But then a guard beckoned for Jack and Annie to leave the throne platform.

Jack and Annie climbed down the steps and returned to their places behind the other ambassadors.

*Wow, wow, wow!* Jack thought. *We did it!*

The Great Mogul stood up from his cushion. Quickly and quietly, he walked down the steps of the Peacock Throne. No one moved as the all-powerful ruler slipped out of the hall.

The whole audience seemed to breathe a sigh of relief. Everyone began talking and moving

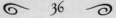

about. The guards stepped forward to escort the ambassadors through the door at the back of the hall.

"Come on, let's get out of here!" Jack whispered to Annie. He pulled her away from the other ambassadors, and they joined the stream of court nobles heading toward the doors at the front of the hall.

"Mission accomplished!" Annie exclaimed. She handed Jack the emerald rose.

Jack stared at the delicately cut stone. It had five tiny rose petals that curled back at the edges. "Great work," he said to Annie. He carefully put the jewel in his bag and buckled it. "I was wrong. You were right."

"I won't rub it in," said Annie with a grin.

"That's okay, I deserve it," Jack said. "I shouldn't have worried so much. Now we just have to get back to the tree house. Keep your head down. Move quickly."

Jack and Annie wound their way through the

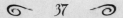

crowd, heading for the front doors. Just as they were about to step into the sunlight, another guard blocked their way.

"Excuse us," said Jack. He tried to step around the guard who towered over them.

But the guard put out his large hand. "I will escort you now to the palace," he said, "to the private balcony of the Great Mogul."

"Uh . . . why?" Jack asked.

"All the ambassadors are to view a parade in their honor," said the guard.

"Parade?" said Annie. "I love parades."

"Uh . . . but we're kind of in a hurry. Do we have a choice?" Jack asked.

"No," said the guard.

"Oh," said Jack. "Okay."

"This way," said the guard.

Jack and Annie walked after him back through the empty hall.

"Don't worry," Annie whispered to Jack. "What could possibly go wrong at a parade?"

## CHAPTER FIVE

# Not Funny

The tall guard escorted Jack and Annie out the back door of the hall and into a walled courtyard. The other ambassadors were already entering the palace quarters on the far side.

Jack was so frustrated he barely noticed the crimson and purple flowers, the bubbling fountains, and the dazzling water pools in the courtyard. All he wanted to do was get back to the tree house. Their mission was done. He tried to think of an excuse to get away.

"Annie!" he whispered.

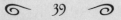

By now Annie was walking ahead and chatting with the guard. "Where do the royal women and children live?" she asked.

The guard pointed to the palace quarters on the left side of the courtyard. Jack noticed veiled women peeping out from behind the arched windows. Annie waved at them, but the women moved out of sight.

The guard escorted Jack and Annie out of the courtyard and through a quiet passageway. The passageway led to a chamber lit with brass lanterns hanging from the wall. The guard handed them each a silk coat, a sash, a pair of pointy shoes, and a jeweled turban.

"Um . . . what's this?" asked Jack.

"Gifts from the Great Mogul. You may change in here," the guard said.

"Oh. Thanks," said Jack.

The guard pulled aside a curtain to reveal a small space like a dressing room. Jack and Annie stepped inside, and the guard pulled the curtain shut.

Jack whirled around to Annie. "This is awful!"

he whispered. "We have to get out of here!"

"Calm down," said Annie. "We don't have a choice." She rubbed her hand over her purple silk coat. "I love these clothes."

"Oh, brother," said Jack, sighing. But he took off his hot jacket and pulled on his orange coat and tied the sash. He definitely felt cooler in the soft silk coat, but the puffy pants made the coat balloon out around his waist. "I really hate this," he groaned.

"Don't worry, we'll leave right after the parade," said Annie. She tucked her braids under her orange turban. "Do I still look like a boy?"

"You look ridiculous," said Jack. "We both look ridiculous. We have to make some excuse so we can leave."

"Don't you want to see the parade?" asked Annie.

"Not with a person who kills you if you speak to him or bow the wrong way," said Jack.

"Maybe we won't have to bow again," said Annie.

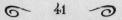

"You're missing my point," said Jack. He put on his blue turban. Then he took off his buckled shoes and pulled on the pointy slippers.

Annie looked at him and laughed.

"Not funny," said Jack.

"Well, don't forget, if we run into trouble, we can always drink the potion and make ourselves small," said Annie.

"And get squashed by the Mogul's guards? No thank you," said Jack.

Annie laughed again.

"Not funny," said Jack.

The imperial guard pushed open the curtain to the dressing room. "Come with me now," he said.

Jack and Annie followed the guard out of the chamber and down a hallway of the palace. "Remember, don't talk to the other ambassadors," whispered Jack. "And never, *ever* say anything to the Great Mogul. Promise?"

"Don't worry, I know what to do," whispered Annie.

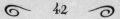

Jack and Annie followed the guard through another chamber and out to a wide, shaded balcony. The balcony overlooked a river and a sandy shore.

The Great Mogul stood near the railing of the balcony, with imperial guards surrounding him. The ambassadors stood in a row behind them. Jack was relieved to see that they, too, were wearing pointy shoes and silk coats that stuck out.

Jack gestured to Annie to stand behind the ambassadors. He hoped none of them would try to talk to him. He was relieved to hear trumpets suddenly blaring and drums booming. All the men stepped forward to watch the parade.

Musicians came first. Hundreds of them marched in formation down the flat sandy shore between the palace and the river. Some blew long golden trumpets. Others beat drums tied around their bodies.

Dozens of flag bearers followed the musicians, their red and yellow banners waving in the hot,

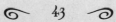

dry wind. After them came row after row of tall, elegant horses with golden bridles. Some were dark gray. Others were copper colored, milk white, or midnight black.

"One hundred Arabian horses!" an imperial guard announced to the ambassadors. "The most beautiful animals in the world!"

Jack glanced at the Great Mogul. The ruler was coldly watching the parade.

Next came carts pulled by white oxen. Riding on the carts were cheetahs with tan fur and black spots. They wore gold collars that glittered in the sunlight.

"One hundred cheetahs!" announced the guard. "The fastest land animals in the world!"

Then came rows and rows of elephants kicking up a sea of dust. They looked like a fleet of gray ships.

"One hundred elephants caught in the wild!" said the guard. "The largest land animals in the world!"

The elephants wore gold chains and silver bells around their necks. The tops of their heads were covered with fancy fringed cloth. On their backs were straw carriages with riders inside.

"Oh, wow, elephants," said Annie, her eyes shining.

"Shhh! We can't talk," whispered Jack.

Elephants, oxen, and horses all stepped in time to the beat of the drums and the blare of the trumpets.

Suddenly the music was interrupted by wild shrieks and bellows.

The Great Mogul, his guards, and the ambassadors all moved to get a better view. Jack and Annie stood on their tiptoes to see what was happening.

Jack could see that an elephant had broken out of line and left the parade. Guards were struggling to capture it. The elephant had reared up on its hind legs, and its rider had tumbled from the carriage on its back. The elephant was making a terrible noise, like a screaming trumpet.

"What's happening? What's making that noise?" said Annie.

"An elephant," whispered Jack.

*"Oh, no!"* said Annie.

Jack grabbed her by the arm. "Don't say anything. Don't do anything," he whispered. "Think of Penny."

"I am! I hate it when animals are hurt!" said Annie. She pulled away from Jack and slipped through the row of ambassadors.

Jack moved after her. "Annie! Come back!" he whispered.

One of the guards saw Annie heading toward the railing where the Great Mogul stood. He quickly stepped in front of her.

"Excuse me, sir, I'm worried about that elephant," Annie said in a low voice. "What's wrong with it?"

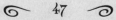

"She tried to escape," the guard said. "They are capturing her now."

"What's going to happen to her?" asked Annie, trying to look around the guard.

"She will be punished," said the guard.

"What?" said Annie. "Why?"

"She has failed to show respect for the Great Mogul," said the guard.

*"What?"* Annie said.

"Annie!" Jack warned.

But Annie didn't seem to hear him. "That's crazy! She's just an animal!" she said to the guard. Her voice was fierce.

"Annie, quiet! Please!" said Jack.

The imperial guards and the other ambassadors were looking at Annie with alarm. Worst of all, the Great Mogul was staring at her, too.

# CHAPTER SIX

# Morning Breeze

"**Y**our Majesty, sir!" Annie called to the Great Mogul. "She's just an animal! Please don't let anyone hurt her!"

"Shhh! You can't talk to him!" Jack whispered furiously.

"Please help her!" Annie said to the Great Mogul. "She doesn't know how great you are. She doesn't know she should respect you."

The Great Mogul kept staring at Annie but said nothing.

"Don't you love animals?" Annie asked.

The Great Mogul didn't answer.

"Don't you love *anything*?" asked Annie.

The ambassadors gasped. Two of the guards grabbed Annie by her arms.

"No, please, she—*he* can't help it!" Jack explained to the guards. "That's just the way my brother is. He can't stop himself from talking. Please, tell your ruler that!"

The Great Mogul murmured something to a bodyguard. Then he turned and left the balcony.

The guard looked startled. He said something in a low voice to the men holding Annie. Jack held his breath. Were they going to drag her away? To his surprise, the guards let Annie go.

"Is the Great Mogul going to punish the elephant?" Annie asked.

"No, he is not," a guard said. "He has given her to you as a gift."

*"What?"* said Jack.

"Really?" said Annie.

"Given her to us as a gift? What does that mean, exactly?" Jack asked.

"It means you must take her home," said the guard. "Back to your own country."

"Take the elephant *home*?" said Jack.

"Come with me," the guard said.

"Come on, Jack!" Annie called as she hurried after the guard, leaving the balcony.

"Take the elephant *home*?" Jack repeated.

The ambassadors were still gaping at him. "Who *are* you?" one of them asked. "Where are you from?"

"Jack, ambassador from Frog Creek," said Jack. "Excuse me." In a daze, he hurried after Annie and the guard. When he caught up to them, he whispered to Annie, "Have you lost your mind? We can't take an elephant home!"

"We can't let her stay here, either," said Annie. "They'll punish her!"

"Okay. Then you can be the one who carries her up the rope ladder," said Jack.

"Ha-ha," said Annie.

"It's not ha-ha," said Jack, "it's insane."

"Look, let's just get her out of the Red Fort first," said Annie. "Then we'll figure out what to do."

Jack and Annie followed the guard until they emerged at the edge of the square in front of the Hall of Public Audience. Several guards were scuffling with the elephant. They had a rope around her neck. Her ears were flapping. She was snorting and stamping her feet.

The guards pulled on the rope, forcing the elephant down on her knees. Her eyes looked desperate and furious.

"Hey, don't hurt her!" Jack blurted out.

A guard pointed his saber at Jack. "Climb on. Now. Both of you," he said. "You have caused enough trouble this day. It is a miracle you are still alive!"

Jack clutched his bag and scrambled awkwardly into the straw carriage on the elephant's back. Annie climbed in behind him. Crammed together, they gripped the sides of the carriage.

"Her name is Morning Breeze!" the guard shouted. "Take her back to your own land! Go now! Before the Great Mogul changes his mind!"

As if obeying the guard, Morning Breeze rose to her full height. She moved quickly across the square and headed down the stone road that led to the gate.

Jack and Annie bounced up and down. They clutched the sides of the straw carriage, trying not to fall out. Jack could hear the guards roaring with laughter behind them. "Slow down!" Jack shouted to the elephant.

But Morning Breeze ran even faster, her big leathery ears flapping and her bells jangling.

"She's more like a wind than a breeze!" shouted Annie.

"More like a tornado!" Jack yelled.

Morning Breeze thundered through the gate and over the wooden drawbridge. Jack and Annie held on to the sides of the carriage for dear life. After she'd crossed the moat, the elephant finally slowed to a walk.

Morning Breeze held her trunk high. She seemed to be sniffing the hot wind. Her ears spread out as if she were listening for a distant sound.

"We're near the tree house! It's right there in that row of trees!" said Jack. "We have the emerald rose. If we can just make her stop, we can jump off and go home. We can get out of this heat and away from this place—"

"I know, I know," said Annie. "But—"

"Stop! Stop, Morning Breeze!" said Jack. "Let us off!"

"But what about *her*?" said Annie. "We can't just leave her here by herself!"

Jack looked at Morning Breeze's trunk waving in the air. He heard what sounded like crying coming from the wild elephant. She seemed terribly lost and sad.

Suddenly Jack wanted desperately to help the elephant get back to the wild, wherever that was. "All right," he said. "Keep going. Go fast!" His voice rose to a shout. "Hurry! Go, Morning Breeze! Go!"

# CHAPTER SEVEN

# Something Very Weird

Her trunk high in the air, Morning Breeze kept sniffing the hot wind.

"We'll get her away from here!" Jack said to Annie. "Then you and I can walk back to the tree house!"

"Great!" said Annie.

"Go!" Jack yelled again at the elephant. "Go home! Go home!" He looked over his shoulder. He was afraid the Great Mogul might change his mind and send his guards after them.

Morning Breeze let out a long, deep rumble and

flapped her ears, as if she'd finally heard a distant call or caught a special scent. Her rumbling cries grew louder and louder—*rrrrrRRRRRR!* She lumbered away from the drawbridge of the Red Fort.

Jack was sure the elephant would start down the street filled with horses and oxcarts. But Morning Breeze headed up the other street, the one that went through the bazaar.

"No, no! Go the other way!" cried Jack.

The elephant began to run. Her flat oval feet thumped against the road as she headed toward the tents and stalls of the bazaar. The street was crowded with merchants and shoppers—bearded men in colorful coats and women in outfits that completely hid their faces and bodies.

"Watch out, everyone!" Annie cried.

As the elephant ran between the busy stalls, everyone scrambled out of her way.

"Sorry! Sorry!" yelled Jack.

"Rogue elephant!" a banana seller shouted.

"Sorry! Sorry!" Jack kept shouting.

Morning Breeze knocked over wooden poles

that supported white tents. The tents collapsed onto burlap bags filled with figs, rice, and peas. She knocked over baskets of lemons, oranges, and pineapples.

Angry merchants yelled and shook their fists.

"She's from the wild! She can't help it!" Annie cried.

"Sorry! Sorry!" Jack said.

Morning Breeze pulled down hanging silk shawls and carpets with her trunk. The silk merchant shouted with rage. He and the other sellers grabbed sticks and charged at the elephant. Jack and Annie scrunched down in their small straw carriage.

"Hurry! Go! Go!" Jack called to Morning Breeze.

With the merchants all chasing after her, Morning Breeze bolted from the bazaar. She started down a narrow pebbled road that soon became a dirt path. She left the bearded merchants shouting angrily in the dust.

Morning Breeze kept running down the path,

passing farms with small mud huts. Sheep and goats bleated and scuttled out of her way. Chickens clucked and scattered.

Her bells jangling wildly, the elephant clomped past women and girls tending outdoor cooking fires. She lumbered past men and boys unloading hay from wooden carts.

"Hi! Hi! Excuse us!" Annie yelled, waving. Jack tried to smile as he clung to the sides of the swaying carriage.

No one smiled or waved back. Everyone stared in shock as the elephant thundered by.

Morning Breeze ran to the end of the dirt path. But she didn't stop there. She kept running, cutting her own path through a sun-scorched field. Jack felt as if they were riding a big gray ship on waves of tall yellow grass.

"This is fun!" said Annie.

*Not really,* thought Jack. Where in the world were they going?

A million insects hummed and buzzed. Butterflies and dragonflies darted about. The elephant burst from the sea of grass and charged into a scrubby forest. As she plowed through shrubs and trees, birds cawed and flapped out of the brush.

"Okay, slow down, Morning Breeze!" yelled Jack. "You're back in the wild, so you can let us off now! We need to—"

Before he could finish, the elephant lifted her trunk and let out a loud shriek. She reared up on her hind legs. Jack and Annie tumbled out of the

carriage. They slid down the elephant's back and fell onto the ground. Morning Breeze shrieked again and tore away through the forest.

Jack and Annie lay in the dirt. They heard the elephant trampling plants and crashing through bushes. They heard her bells jangling. Then the sounds faded away.

"Are you okay?" Annie asked.

"Yep," said Jack. "But that wasn't very polite of her."

Annie laughed. "Well, you asked her to let us off," she said.

"Yeah, but not *dump* us off," said Jack. He waved away flies and slapped at mosquitoes. He felt sweaty and thirsty and exhausted. "I wonder how long it will take us to get back to the tree house?"

"I don't know—let's just start retracing our steps," said Annie.

Jack and Annie stood up and brushed the dirt off their coats.

"Hey, where's your bag?" asked Annie.

"My bag?" said Jack. Where was it? He whirled around. He saw it lying in the grass.

"There!" he said. He hurried to his bag and picked it up. It was open. "Oh, no!" He reached in and pulled out their research book, the blue bottle, and Teddy and Kathleen's note. He searched frantically for the emerald rose.

"I don't believe it! The emerald's missing!" cried Jack.

"It must have slipped out when we fell off Morning Breeze," said Annie. "We'll find it. It has to be here somewhere."

Jack shoved everything back into his bag. Then he and Annie got down on their hands and knees. Jack looked intently at the forest undergrowth— the dried vegetation, sticks, clumps of dirt, and rotten leaves.

"I can't believe this!" said Jack. They had been so close to returning home, their mission done. Now they were stuck in the middle of nowhere and the emerald rose was missing. "I don't see it. It's not here. Maybe it fell out at the bazaar when—"

"Bingo!" said Annie. "There it is!"

"Where? Where?" said Jack.

"There!" Annie said, pointing.

Jack saw it. The emerald rose glittered like a tiny green light in a small, sunlit clearing. It was lying next to a mound of earth and dead leaves.

"Yes!" said Jack. He and Annie scrambled to their feet and headed for the mound.

But when they got closer, Annie grabbed his arm. "Wait! There's something weird happening there," she whispered. "*Very* weird. See?"

"What? Where?" said Jack.

Annie pointed to the mound. Something very weird *was* happening. The earth and leaves seemed to be moving! Then Jack saw speckled yellow bands and two shiny black eyes.

Jack gasped. "Oh, no," he whispered. "A king cobra!"

## CHAPTER EIGHT

# SHHHHHH-WISSSSSST!

The king cobra circled the leafy mound. Its skin was olive brown, the color of the dead leaves. It had speckled yellow bands that ran around its scaly body.

"Back up, back up. Go slow," Jack whispered to Annie. Jack picked up his bag, and they quietly stepped backward, until they got to the edge of the clearing. "Now run!"

Jack and Annie took off. Clutching his bag, Jack ran with little steps, trying not to lose his pointy slippers. After about a hundred yards,

Annie came to a halt. "Stop, stop!" She grabbed Jack's arm. "We shouldn't get too far away!"

"Why not?" said Jack.

"Penny!" said Annie. "We have to get the emerald for Penny!"

"Right, right," said Jack. "Okay!" He took a deep breath. "First, we have to get calm." Jack took another deep breath. Then he pulled out their research book. "Okay. Let's read about cobras."

Jack opened the book and found a section about Indian wildlife. He read:

> **The king cobra is one of the only snakes known to make a nest for its eggs. The nest is made of a mound of dead leaves. The cobra's scaly skin is the same color as the leaves, a good example of natural camouflage.**

"So that mound of leaves was its nest," said Jack. "And the cobra was probably a mother snake guarding her eggs."

"How does that information help us?" said Annie.

"It doesn't," said Jack. He went on:

> King cobras cannot hear, but they have excellent vision and can feel vibrations. They will attack anything they see that gets too close to their nests.

"That's bad news," said Annie.

"Yep, really bad news," said Jack. He kept reading:

> When threatened, the king cobra flattens its neck into a hood. A single bite from the snake contains enough venom to kill twenty men or a large elephant.

"Whoa," said Annie. "That must be why Morning Breeze panicked and ran away."

Jack closed the book. He shook his head. "I don't see how we can possibly get close to that nest," he said.

"Then there's no way we can get an emerald rose for Penny," said Annie, "unless we go back to the Great Mogul and ask for another one."

"And that's not going to happen," said Jack.

"Then how can we save Penny?" asked Annie. "Think of Penny."

Jack thought about Penny. He would do anything for her. "Okay," he said. "There might be a way we could get the emerald rose. What if . . . what if we were really small?"

"*Yes!*" said Annie.

"The cobra can't hear us, right?" said Jack. "She can only see us and feel vibrations. So if we make ourselves small, maybe we can sneak back and get the emerald without being seen."

"*Yes!*" said Annie.

Jack reached into his bag and pulled out the blue bottle. He and Annie both stared at it. "So how many sips should we take?" Jack asked. "One for ten minutes?"

Annie shook her head. "Two for twenty."

"Okay . . ." Jack took a deep breath. "But just

so you know, when we get small, everything else will be huge, like flies and spiders and—"

"Spiders?" Annie said in a small voice.

"Yeah," said Jack. "Hey, you know what? You don't have to do this. I can do it by myself. It only takes one person to get the emerald."

"No! *I'll* go. *You* stay," said Annie.

"No way," said Jack. "We'll both go."

"Good," said Annie.

Jack held the bottle up to his lips. "Okay," he said, "two sips." He took two quick sips, then handed the bottle to Annie.

Jack felt dizzy. He closed his eyes and hugged himself. He felt as if he were falling through a hole.

*SHHHHHH-WISSSSSST!*

Suddenly the forest was filled with chirping, whirring, crunching, and squeaking.

"Oh, wow!" whispered Annie. "Open your eyes."

Jack opened his eyes.

He and Annie were both small—*very* small. Their clothes and shoes and Jack's bag were all small, too.

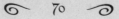

"Oh, man, we got *really* small," said Jack. He looked around at the grass and the weeds and the mushrooms—they were all taller than he was! "I think we shrunk to about six or eight inches."

Close to the ground, the scrubby forest was awake and alive, filled with the ripe smells of earth, noisy insect sounds, and the rustling and whispering of grasses and weeds. The dirt glittered as if sprinkled with flecks of silver.

"It's really beautiful," said Annie.

"Yeah . . . ," said Jack.

Wildflowers looked like elegant and luminous umbrellas with pale pink petals and silvery leaves. Berries were the size of apples.

"Look up!" said Annie.

"Wow!" said Jack.

The tall trees of the forest were like skyscrapers. It was hard to see where they ended.

*WHUP!* Something plopped down in the dirt beside Jack.

"AHHH!" Jack and Annie grabbed each other in terror.

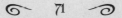

It was a giant insect—as long as Jack's arm! It had a flat brown body, six legs, and two sets of wings. It looked at them with huge, goggle-like eyes. It waved its antennae and crept forward.

"AHHH!" Jack and Annie stumbled backward.

The giant bug stopped. Then it rubbed its front wings together. The forest erupted with shrill chirping—*Creekle! CREEKLE! Creekle! CREEKLE!*

Jack covered his ears and laughed. The giant insect was a cricket! He knew a cricket wouldn't hurt them. The cricket pushed off the ground with its long hind legs and leapt into the brush.

"Look!" said Annie, glancing up.

A giant golden yellow butterfly hovered above her. As if Annie were a flower, the butterfly touched down lightly on her head and opened its wings. Annie held her breath. She didn't move a muscle. She looked like she was wearing a wide yellow hat.

The butterfly closed its wings, then opened

them, and with a whispery sound, fluttered deeper into the forest.

*Bzzzzzzzzzzz-zzzzzzzzzz.*

A gigantic bee circled above Jack. "Whoa. Keep moving, buddy!" Jack said, ducking and waving his hands. "We're not flowers!"

The bee buzzed lazily away.

"Hey, we'd better hurry and get our emerald before we become our *real* size again," said Annie.

"Oh, right!" said Jack.

"Which way?" asked Annie.

Jack looked around. It was hard to tell where they were. "I remember the emerald was shining in the sunlight."

"It looks sunny over there," said Annie. She pointed to a clearing.

"So let's creep through the shade toward the light," said Jack. "Remember, the cobra can't hear us, but she can see us and feel our vibrations. We have to stay hidden and step lightly."

"Hey, I wonder where the dad is," said Annie.

"Don't ask," said Jack. "Don't think about it. We have enough to worry about. Come on. Let's go."

He and Annie crouched down and started creeping toward the sunlight.

# CHAPTER NINE

## Camouflage

Jack and Annie stepped lightly through dead leaves and pushed aside feathery weeds that towered above them. They carefully climbed over twigs, pebbles, and tangled roots. They skirted around a deserted anthill as high as Jack's knees.

When they got to the edge of the cobra's clearing, Jack stopped. He held up his hand and Annie nodded. They peered between tall blades of grass.

The emerald rose glittered in the sunlight. It looked as big as a softball. The cobra was still coiled around her nest. But now she looked as big as a monster in a fairy tale.

"Whoa!" Jack breathed.

"What do you think we should do?" Annie whispered. "Should I just run as fast as I can, grab it, and run back?"

"No, no!" said Jack. He was shocked by how big the cobra looked.

"I think she's asleep," said Annie.

"We can't really tell," said Jack. "Her eyes are hard to see because of her camouflage."

"So how—" started Annie.

"That's it!" said Jack. *"Camouflage!"*

"What about it?" said Annie.

"That's how we'll get the emerald!" said Jack. "We'll use our own camouflage."

"You mean like leaves?" said Annie.

"Yeah, leaves would be good," said Jack. They looked around. "There." He pointed to a vine with large light green leaves. He and Annie gripped one of the leaves and pulled until it tore off the vine.

Annie held it up in front of her like a shield. "How's this?" she said.

"Great," said Jack. "Now one for me." He and Annie gripped another leaf and pulled until they ripped it from the vine, too.

"Poke holes in them, so we can see," said Annie.

"Good idea," said Jack. They poked holes in their leaves and then held them up, covering their faces. Jack moved his leaf around until he could see the emerald through the eyeholes.

"Go slowly and stick with me," Jack said. "Two steps, then stop. Two steps, then stop."

"Got it," said Annie.

Holding their leaves in front of them, Jack and Annie carefully stepped into the clearing. They took two steps toward the emerald, then stopped . . . two steps, then stopped.

The cobra didn't move. Jack desperately hoped she was asleep. He and Annie took two more steps, then stopped. The emerald glittered in the hot sunlight. They took two more steps. Then Annie gasped.

The cobra was lifting her body above her nest!

Her head was broad and flat. She swayed back and forth and looked around with staring eyes.

Jack and Annie froze.

Then slowly the cobra lowered her head. Jack let out his breath. Their camouflage had worked! He motioned to Annie, and they both took another two steps, then stopped.

Jack was only a step away from the jewel now. Holding up his leaf camouflage with one hand, he leaned over and scooped up the emerald. It felt as heavy as a big rock. Holding the leaf with one hand, Jack used his other hand to shove the emerald into his bag. With Annie behind him, he stepped backward—two steps, then stopped.

Jack kept his eye on the cobra coiled around her nest. He and Annie kept backing up.

Suddenly a sound came from behind them—a strange hissing, growling sound. A chill went through Jack. He turned around.

A monster-size cobra towered over them.

"The dad!" yelled Annie.

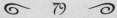

The male cobra had the same coloring as the female. His hood was spread out as he raised himself high above the grass. He swayed from side to side, staring down at Jack and Annie with cold, unblinking eyes. He opened his giant mouth, showing two deadly fangs.

"AHHH!" said Jack and Annie.

They dropped their leaves and crouched down, hiding themselves in the grass. "Go—go!" sputtered Jack. They took off, scrambling through the undergrowth of the forest.

Jack led the way as they both half crawled, half ran over the dirt and through the grass. Jack lost his slippers and ripped his coat. Like a mouse, he clambered over sticks and twigs, nuts, seeds, bark, feathers, mosses, and mushrooms. All kinds of ants and beetles scuttled out of the way. The air was filled with screeching insect sounds.

Jack had no idea where he was running, but he knew he couldn't stop. He was sure the cobra was slithering after them, thrashing through the undergrowth. Maybe *both* king cobras were searching for them now, he thought, and all the forest was screaming about it.

Jack stumbled over a stick. He scrambled up from the dirt and looked around wildly. Where was Annie? He didn't see her! Had she gone off in another direction? Where were the cobras? Had they chased after Annie instead of him?

Jack panicked. "Annie!" he shouted.

The ground trembled. Jack heard thumping, thrashing, and bells. He crouched down in the grass and covered his head. He heard Annie shout, "Jack! Where are you, Jack?" She sounded as if she was up in a tree! What was going on?

Jack looked up. Suddenly a gigantic snake dropped down in front of him.

"AHHH!" Jack yelled.

"Yay!" Annie yelled from overhead.

The snake didn't have the olive brown skin of a cobra. It was gray and wrinkled. It wasn't a snake at all! It was the trunk of an elephant!

Before Jack could think, the tip of the elephant's trunk curled around him. Clutching him like a banana, Morning Breeze lifted Jack up in the air. Jack clung to his bag so he wouldn't lose the emerald again. The trunk curled back, and Jack could see the sky whirling above him.

The elephant uncoiled her trunk and let go of Jack. He plopped down into the straw carriage. Annie was already there!

"Morning Breeze!" Annie cried. "She came back for us!"

Jack was so small, he couldn't see over the sides of the carriage. He tried to stand up to look for the cobras. But just then Morning Breeze bellowed and bolted through the forest. Jack lost his balance and fell backward.

Jack and Annie both laughed as they bounced around in the basket on the back of the elephant. They were safe from the cobras! They had their emerald rose! And Morning Breeze had risked her life to save them!

*SHHHHHH-WISSSSSST!*

## CHAPTER TEN

# Caught in the Wild

Instantly the straw carriage felt small and cramped. Jack and Annie sat up and looked at each other.

"We're big again," said Annie.

"Yeah," said Jack, dazed.

"Where's the emerald?" said Annie.

Jack opened his bag. The jewel looked tiny again, but it was there. "No problem. I have it," he said.

"It was kind of fun being so little, wasn't it?" said Annie.

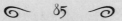

"Yeah, until we nearly got killed by humongous, superpoisonous snakes," said Jack.

"Thanks for saving us, Morning Breeze!" called Annie. She reached out from the carriage and patted the elephant's wrinkled skin.

"Yeah, thanks," said Jack.

Morning Breeze made a trumpet sound and swayed from side to side as she tramped through the low, scraggly brush.

"I wonder where she's going," said Jack.

The elephant slowed down. She sniffed the air with the tip of her trunk. Then she stopped near a clump of bushes and made a low purring sound.

A snuffling noise came from behind the bushes. Branches and leaves shook and parted.

"Ohhhh, *wow!*" breathed Annie.

A baby elephant bumbled out into the open. He had a fuzzy head and bright, shining eyes.

Morning Breeze lowered herself onto her knees. She stretched out her trunk and stroked her baby. The little elephant nuzzled against her.

"So *that's* why Morning Breeze had to escape

the fort!" said Annie. "When they captured her in the wild, they took her away from her baby. She was desperate to get back to him."

"Yeah," said Jack, "and after she found him, she came back to help us."

Annie climbed out of the straw carriage and carefully slid down off the elephant's back. Jack followed her.

Annie patted the elephant's back. "I guess you'll be staying here now that you've found your baby."

Jack rubbed his hand over Morning Breeze's skin. Her huge, wrinkled body smelled of grass and heat and trees. The elephant actually looked as if she were smiling.

"I don't think you need to wear this stuff anymore," said Annie. She reached up and lifted the rope of silver bells off the elephant's neck. The bells jangled as Annie dropped them into the grass.

"Or this," said Jack. He took the fringed cloth off the elephant's head.

"And especially this," said Annie. Together she and Jack unbuckled the strap that held the straw carriage in place on Morning Breeze's back. They pulled the carriage off and set it on the grass.

"Doesn't that feel better?" said Jack.

Morning Breeze stared at Jack and Annie. Her eyes were bright and clear. She trumpeted and rose to her full height.

"Before you go, can we pet your baby?" asked Annie.

The large elephant didn't seem to mind as Annie reached out and stroked the baby elephant. "Whoa," Annie breathed. "Pet him, Jack."

Jack rubbed his hand slowly over the baby's head. The elephant's fuzzy hair felt coarse and tickly. Jack laughed.

"Enjoy being home in the wild again," Annie said to Morning Breeze. "Jack and I have to go back to *our* home now."

"Thanks, Morning Breeze," said Jack. "Good luck."

"We love you," said Annie.

Morning Breeze flapped her ears and waved her trunk at them. Then she turned and lumbered off with her baby at her heels. The two of them kicked up grass and dirt as they disappeared into the brush.

"Wow," said Annie.

"Yeah," said Jack.

Annie turned to Jack and laughed. "We look like we've been in a train wreck," she said.

"No kidding," said Jack. They'd both lost their pointy shoes, and their coats were torn and dirty.

"At least we have our emerald rose," said Annie. "And Morning Breeze is back with her baby."

"Mission done," said Jack.

"So let's go back to the tree house," said Annie.

"Yeah," said Jack. He looked around. "But . . . where the heck are we?"

"I think the big field we came through is over

there," said Annie, pointing. "I hear a lot of bug noise. Let's look."

Jack and Annie headed for the field. "Oww! Oww!" Weeds and rocks jabbed their bare feet. Jack just missed stepping on a large anthill. He and Annie picked their way through the scrubby forest, until they came to the edge of the yellow field.

The sounds of buzzing and chirping filled the air. The tall grasses rustled in the dry, hot wind.

"That's it," said Jack. "So to get back to the tree house, we cross the field, then go on the dirt path, then head back through the bazaar and down the road to the Red Fort. Got it?"

"Got it," said Annie.

"I just hope we don't get eaten alive by bugs," said Jack, "or get heatstroke or get clobbered by those angry guys in the bazaar or—"

"Enough, stop," said Annie, grinning. "One thing at a time. Come on, don't be chicken. The bugs are more afraid of us than we are of them. Run!"

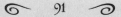

Annie and Jack started running through the dry, dusty field. Their torn silk coats billowed behind them. Jack could feel grasshoppers and all sorts of buzzy and jumpy things bashing against him, but nothing really hurt. His feet crushed the dry, tough grass, until he and Annie finally reached the dirt path.

"Yes! We—we made it!" Annie said, out of breath. "Oh! Look . . ."

Jack was burning up. He felt dizzy. "Whew, we—"

*"Look!"* Annie said again. She grabbed Jack and pointed to a farmer hauling hay. The farmer was talking to an imperial guard in a horse-drawn carriage. It was the same guard who had escorted them to the Great Mogul's balcony!

The farmer pointed back at Jack and Annie. The guard turned and saw them.

"Oh, no! He must be searching for us," said Jack. "Hide!"

But it was too late. The guard had jumped out

of the carriage. He was striding toward the edge of the field. "Stop, ambassadors from Frog Creek!" he called.

Jack held his breath as he and Annie waited for the guard.

The guard looked about as he approached them. "Where is the elephant?" he asked.

"She threw us off," said Annie.

"Yeah, and then she ran that way," said Jack. He pointed to the right, while Annie pointed to the left.

But the guard didn't seem to care about the elephant, nor did he seem to care about their bare feet and torn coats. "You must come with me," he said gruffly.

"Why?" asked Jack.

The guard wrapped his hand around the hilt of his sword. "Because if you do *not*, you will be put in jail for the rest of your lives," he said.

"Oh," said Jack. "Good reason."

## CHAPTER ELEVEN

## Heart to Heart

Jack and Annie silently followed the guard to his carriage and climbed in the back. The guard flicked the reins, and the pair of black horses took off, trotting down the dirt path.

Annie looked at Jack. "I wonder where we're going," she whispered.

Jack just shook his head. His worst thought was that the Great Mogul had changed his mind and wanted to punish them.

The horses passed the mud huts, the men and boys hauling hay, the women and girls cooking outdoors. They passed goats and sheep and chickens.

The horses clopped down the stone road. They moved easily through the bazaar. Jack saw that the silks and carpets were hanging on the lines again. Oranges, lemons, and pineapples were back in the baskets. Tent poles were all standing, and the bearded merchants looked happy and busy.

The horses trotted down the street toward the Red Fort. When they came to the drawbridge, Jack expected them to cross the moat and head back to the palace, but they didn't. The horses trotted past the fort and down a road along the river.

The sun was low in the sky when the horse-drawn carriage came to a square. The horses stopped before a massive red gateway with an arched entrance.

The guard turned to Jack and Annie. "You are to go inside and wait," he said.

"Okay. Thanks for the ride," said Annie.

The guard stayed in the carriage while Jack and Annie climbed out. They walked up to the looming gateway.

"Where are we?" Annie whispered to Jack. "And why are we here?"

"If I knew, I'd tell you," whispered Jack.

Jack and Annie stepped under the high, arched entrance. Leading from the entrance was a narrow canal stretching to the horizon.

In the sunset, Jack thought he saw a cloud of mist hovering above the ground. Then he realized it was a shimmering, milky white dome about twenty stories high. It seemed to float between the earth and the sky. There were four tall towers at the corners of a terrace beneath the dome.

Jack and Annie just stared at the dreamlike vision. Then they saw a man walking along the narrow canal toward them. As the man got closer, Jack caught his breath. It was the Great Mogul! No guards were with him. He was all alone.

The Great Mogul stopped and stared at them. His gaze took in their ragged, torn coats and bare feet.

Jack panicked. They looked terrible. Would the

ruler think they weren't showing proper respect for him?

"Bow," Annie whispered.

Together, they bowed from their waists and brushed their right hands on the ground. They straightened up, raised their right hands into the air, and placed their palms on their heads. Then they lowered their hands and stood perfectly still. Jack cast his eyes down, afraid to look directly at the Great Mogul.

There was a moment of silence. Then the all-powerful ruler spoke. "I have never read such writing before. Or seen such artwork," he said.

Jack looked up at the Great Mogul. But he didn't know what to do. Were they allowed to talk?

"Excuse me, Your Majesty," said Annie. "Is it all right to speak?"

"Yes," said the Great Mogul.

"Thank you. Well, Jack wrote the words," said Annie. "And I drew the pictures."

The Great Mogul nodded. "Your story and

pictures tell of riding through the world in a tree house. You tell of saving a huge octopus, a baby gorilla, and a baby kangaroo. You tell of helping brilliant men named Leonardo da Vinci and William Shakespeare. You tell of rescuing children from a giant ocean wave and from a sinking ship. You are a great storyteller," he said to Jack.

"Oh, not really," said Jack. He felt embarrassed. "I just told about stuff that happened to us."

The Great Mogul turned to Annie. "Your pictures are filled with life and joy. They are rich and stirring. You are a great artist," he said.

"Not really," Annie said. "Lots of people draw better than me. What you probably loved was the perfect printing of Jack's story and the sparkly colors of my pens."

"Yeah, we can't take credit for those things," said Jack.

The Great Mogul almost smiled. "The perfect letters and the sparkles were not what I liked best," he said. "I liked the heart in the story. I liked the heart in the drawings."

Jack couldn't explain why, but he thought he understood what the Great Mogul meant.

"And now I want to answer the question you asked me today," the Great Mogul said to Annie. "You asked if I loved anything. I could not speak freely in front of my guards or my foreign guests. But the answer is yes. I once did love something—some*one*—very much. My wife. She was my best friend and the mother of many children. I wept an ocean of tears when she died."

"Oh. I'm so sorry," said Annie.

"Me too," said Jack.

"You have shown me your hearts," said the Great Mogul. "Now I show you mine." He turned and looked at the shimmering dome. "This is the tomb of marble I built for my wife. It is called the Taj Mahal."

# CHAPTER TWELVE

# The Meaning of the Emerald

Jack, Annie, and the Great Mogul were silent for a long moment. The marble of the Taj Mahal seemed to change color as the sun went down. Against the darkening sky, it went from pale pink to orange to purple. The dome sparkled as if it were covered with a thousand tiny lights.

"How did you make it sparkle like that?" Annie asked finally.

"Stonecutters set precious stones in the marble," said the Great Mogul. "Many were cut in the shapes of flowers and leaves. The emerald rose you chose today is like the carved flowers set in the Taj Mahal."

"It's really beautiful," Jack said.

"Yes. Many say it is the most beautiful building in all the world," said the Great Mogul. "But hidden beneath the sparkle and magnificence of the Taj Mahal is simply the lonely heart of one person who loved another." The Great Mogul had tears in his eyes. He cleared his throat and looked away from them. "And the elephant I gave you—where is she now?"

"Uh . . . actually . . . ," Jack started. He didn't know what to say. How could he protect Morning Breeze?

"We left her in the forest," Annie finished. "She has a baby she wanted to take care of. You

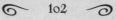

102

probably didn't know this, but Morning Breeze was a new mom when she was captured. She's a good mother. She should stay with her baby."

The Great Mogul nodded. "I understand," he said. "My wife was a good mother, too. The last thing she said to me was 'Please take care of our children.' Do not worry, the elephant will remain in the forest with her child."

"Thank you," said Annie.

The Great Mogul stared at them for a long moment. When he spoke again, his voice was kind. "You are ambassadors from far away," he said, "but you are children, too. You should go back to your home, to those who care for you."

"A splendid idea," said Jack, trying to sound like an ambassador.

"Come." The Great Mogul walked with Jack and Annie back to the arched entrance and through the tall gate. He waved at the driver in the cart. Then he turned to Jack and Annie.

"Farewell," he said. "Travel safely."

"Thank you," said Annie.

"Bow," Jack whispered to her.

Jack and Annie performed their bow one last time. When they straightened up, the Great Mogul nodded.

"Oh, and thank you for the emerald rose," said Annie. "It is a priceless treasure."

"You are most welcome," said the Great Mogul. "The rose was my wife's favorite flower. And, as you know, emeralds stand for love." For the first time, a warm smile crossed his face.

Jack and Annie smiled back at him.

But the Great Mogul was suddenly serious again, as if he wasn't allowed to smile. He looked at Jack and Annie for a moment. Then, without another word, he turned and walked through the tall gate, back toward the shimmering tomb of his wife.

Jack looked at Annie. "Let's go home now," he said.

Jack and Annie walked to the guard and his horse-drawn carriage. "Please take us to the trees outside the walls of the Red Fort," Jack said.

The guard flicked his reins. The black horses trotted along the river in the pink twilight. They passed veiled women on the backs of elephants, white oxen pulling a cart, and small boys driving a herd of sheep. They stopped near the row of dark trees outside the Red Fort.

"This is fine. We'll get out here, please," said Jack.

The guard gave them a silent nod.

Jack and Annie jumped out of the cart. They ran under the trees to the rope ladder and climbed into the tree house. Jack grabbed the Pennsylvania book. Before he made the wish, he and Annie looked out the window.

In the distance, they could just see the Taj Mahal. It glowed faintly in the hot night, like a shimmering cloud.

"Oh, wait . . . ," said Jack. "I just remembered something." He reached into his bag and pulled out the note from Kathleen and Teddy. He read aloud:

*Ye say that ye wish
your spell be reversed?
Four things ye must find.
Here is the first:*

*In the shape of a rose
is an emerald stone
that uncovers the heart
of one who's alone.*

Jack put the note away. "Our mission wasn't really done until now," he said. "We were so worried about the emerald rose, we forgot the part about uncovering the heart of one who's alone."

"The Great Mogul," said Annie. "Even though he has millions of followers, he's really lonely."

Jack and Annie looked out the window again. "Good-bye, Great Mogul," Annie said. "I hope your heart feels better someday."

Jack took a deep breath. He pointed at a picture of the Frog Creek woods. "I wish we could go home," he said.

The wind began to blow.

The tree house started to spin.

It spun faster and faster.

Then everything was still.

Absolutely still.

❖ ❖ ❖

Jack and Annie were wearing their own clothes again. Jack's bag was a backpack. A warm wind was blowing the trees in the Frog Creek woods.

"I'm glad it's not boiling hot here," said Jack.

"It feels good," said Annie. "You've still got the emerald rose, right?"

Jack looked in his backpack. "Got it," he said. He pulled out their note, their research book, and the blue bottle, and he left them in the corner of the tree house.

Then Jack took out the sparkling stone and held it up to the afternoon light. "This is for you, Penny," Jack said. "We'll take this home and keep it safe until we see Teddy and Kathleen again."

"Good," said Annie.

Jack carefully put the emerald rose back into his backpack. Then he looked at Annie. "Home," he said.

Jack and Annie climbed down the rope ladder. As they walked through the Frog Creek woods, Annie was unusually quiet.

"What's on your mind?" Jack asked.

"Well, I was just thinking that it's really cool that emeralds stand for love," said Annie. "Love was the reason for every big thing that happened today."

"How do you mean?" said Jack. He thought their day had been crazy.

"Well, we went on our mission because Merlin—and everyone else in Camelot—loves Penny," said Annie, "and we love her, too."

"Right . . . ," said Jack.

"And the Great Mogul gave us Morning Breeze because I loved her," said Annie.

"Right," said Jack.

"And Morning Breeze took us into the wild because she loved her baby," said Annie.

"Right," said Jack.

"And we ran into trouble with the cobras because they loved their babies-to-be," said Annie.

"Yeah . . . ," said Jack. "Okay."

"And finally, the Great Mogul showed us the Taj Mahal, which is the most amazing building we've ever seen, and he built it because he loved his wife," said Annie.

"Yeah," said Jack. "You're right." Annie made it all sound so simple.

"And now I would love to go home," said Annie.

"Me too," said Jack.

"Hey, we can tell Mom and Dad you got an A plus on your story," said Annie. "We'll print it out again."

"Yeah, and I made copies of your artwork," said Jack. "Except the sparkles don't really show."

"That's okay," said Annie. "The sparkles aren't that important."

"Right," said Jack. "It's the heart that counts." And the two of them left the Frog Creek woods and headed home under the cloudless May sky.

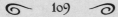

# Author's Note

## Taj Mahal

Shah Jahān, the Great Mogul whose name means "king of the world," ruled the Mogul Empire of India from 1628 to 1658. Shah Jahān was a ruthless king, but he was also a supporter of writing, painting, and astonishing architecture. And he left behind many buildings, mosques, and beautiful gardens.

Shah Jahān's favorite wife was Mumtāz Mahal, who bore him fourteen children. After she died, he built a mausoleum, or large tomb, in her memory. The mausoleum was called the Taj Mahal, which means "crown palace."

It took over twenty years to finish the Taj

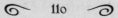

Mahal. Twenty thousand men from all over the Mogul Empire worked on it, using small hand tools to split the marble stone. Artisans set precious gems into the marble to make flowers. A court poet wrote:

*They set stone flowers in the marble*
*that by their color, if not their perfume,*
*surpass real flowers.*

A Russian visitor in the late 1800s wrote that the flowers looked so natural that you wanted to touch them to make sure they weren't real. He said that "every leaf, every petal is a separate emerald, pearl or topaz" (Diana and Michael Preston in *Taj Mahal*, p. 190).

### Asian Elephants

There are two different kinds of elephants: Asian and African. Asian elephants have smaller ears than African elephants, their skin is not quite as wrinkly, and their backs are dome-shaped. Both species are endangered because their habitats are shrinking and poachers are illegally hunting them for the ivory in their tusks.

An Asian elephant uses its trunk not only to smell, but also to drink water and to wipe its eyes, as well as to play and grapple with other elephants. And it uses the trunk as a sort of finger that can coil around food and lift it up to the elephant's mouth.

## King Cobras

King cobras, the largest venomous snakes in the world, can be eighteen feet long. A king cobra can lift up to one-third of its body into the air—which means that an eighteen-foot-long cobra can rise six feet off the ground!

# Turn the page for
# great activities!

# Fun Activities for Jack and Annie and *You*!

## Egg-Carton Snake

In *A Crazy Day with Cobras*, Jack and Annie come face to face with king cobras. Make your own colorfully patterned snake, and see what kind of adventures you get into!

You will need:

- Cardboard egg carton
- Scissors
- Paint (any colors you choose)
- Paintbrush
- Yarn or ribbon
- Red ribbon or red construction paper
- Two googly eyes, two buttons, or markers
- Glue

1. Cut out five cups from the cardboard egg carton.

2. Trim the rims of each cup so that they have smooth edges.

3. Set one cup aside—this will be the snake's head. Turn each of the other four cups upside down to look like hats. These four cups are the snake's body.

4. Paint the four cups to give the snake decorative scales. Let dry.

5. Set the cup that is the snake's head on its side. Paint the outside, and paint the inside to give the snake a mouth. Let dry.

6. Ask an adult to use the scissors to punch one hole in the back of the snake's mouth, and a hole in the front and the back of each cup. This will allow you to string the cups together.

7. Tie each cup to the next using yarn or ribbon. Now your snake can slither.

8. Cut the red ribbon or red construction paper to look like a snake's tongue. Glue it into the snake's mouth.

9. Give the snake eyes by gluing on buttons or googly eyes. You can also draw eyes with markers.

10. Pull your snake to make it wiggle and slither!

# Puzzle of the Elephant

Jack and Annie learned many new things on their adventure in India. Answer the following questions to put your knowledge of *A Crazy Day with Cobras* to the test.

You can use a notebook or make a copy of this page if you don't want to write in your book.

1. Jack and Annie must find an emerald stone shaped like a _ _ _ _.

☐ ☐ ☐ ○

2. The king cobra is one of the only snakes known to make a _ _ _ _ for its eggs.

☐ ☐ ○ ☐

3. What do Jack and Annie pretend to be to meet the Great Mogul?

☐ ○ ☐ ☐ ☐ ☐ ☐ ☐ ☐ ☐ ☐

4. The Great Mogul built the famous Taj _ _ _ _ _ to honor his wife.

☐ ○ ☐ ☐ ☐

5. The Great Mogul gives Annie an

_ _ _ _ _ _ _ _.

□ ○ □ □ □ □ □ □

6. Annie names the elephant _ _ _ _ _ _ _ _
Breeze.

□ □ ○ □ □ □ □

7. What feeling do emeralds stand for?

○ □ □ □

Now look at your answers above. The letters that are circled spell a word—but that word is scrambled! Can you unscramble the letters to complete the final puzzle?

What is one way that you can you tell an Asian elephant from an African elephant? Asian elephants have _ _ _ _ _ _ _ ears.

# Here's a special preview of
## Magic Tree House® Fact Tracker
### Snakes and Other Reptiles

After their adventure in India, Jack and Annie
wanted to find out more about snakes and other
reptiles. Track down the facts with them!

## Available now!

# Snakes

For thousands of years, people have both feared and respected snakes. Many believed they possessed magical powers. Some cultures created myths and legends about them. In ancient Greece, snakes were a symbol of healing and wisdom.

At times, snakes were even worshipped. In ancient Egypt, cobras were considered gods. There and elsewhere, people built temples to honor certain snakes. According to Hindu legend, the god Vishnu often rests on the coils of a giant cobra. Temples to snake gods still exist in India today. People often bring offerings of flowers and food for the snake gods.

## Habitats

The place where an animal or plant lives is its *habitat*. Because they're cold-blooded, snakes don't have habitats in the Arctic or Antarctica. There are also no snakes in Ireland, Iceland, Greenland, and New Zealand. Otherwise, there are snakes all over the world.

Hey, wait a minute! There are no snakes native to Hawaii!

Snakes live in deserts, woods, fields, and rain forests. Green mambas and other snakes spend most of their lives in trees. Some of the largest snakes, such as anacondas and pythons, live near water deep in the rain forests.

Some snakes live in remote places. The rare Tibetan spring snake lives high in the mountains of Tibet near two hot springs. Sea snakes swim deep in the waters of the Pacific and Indian Oceans.

## Snake Skin

When molting, snakes rub their noses over rough surfaces such as rocks or logs to loosen their skin. Except in very large snakes, the skin slips off in one piece like a glove. Many snakes are gray, olive green, and brown. Their dull colors blend into the background and protect them from predators.

An eggeater snake shed this skin in one piece.

Some snakes' skins, such as the diamond python's, have beautiful patterns. There are also snakes with brilliant yellow, green, or red skins. The emerald tree boa in the rain forests of South America has a shimmering green skin that catches the light. Coral snakes in Florida and Arizona sport bright bands of red, black, and yellow or white.

## Movement
Snakes use their muscles and the scales on their bellies to get around. Depending on the species and the surface, snakes move in

different ways. In the case of pythons, boas, and other heavy snakes, their muscles push their bodies forward. The scales on their bellies grip the ground and keep them moving ahead.

A few desert snakes, such as some rattlesnakes, slither across the smooth sand in a sideways motion called *sidewinding*.

Sidewinding snakes sometimes leave prints like these in the sand behind them.

*Don't miss Magic Tree House® #46*
*(A Merlin Mission)*
## Dogs in the Dead of Night

**When Jack and Annie journey to the Swiss Alps, they must help a young Saint Bernard named Barry and avoid avalanches!**

**Available now!**